THE LITTLE MERMAID

Adapted by FREYA LITTLEDALE
from the story by Hans Christian Andersen

Illustrated by DANIEL SAN SOUCI

SCHOLASTIC INC.

New York   Toronto   London   Auckland   Sydney

ISBN 0-590-44358-5

Text copyright © 1986 by Freya Littledale. Illustrations copyright © 1986 by Daniel San Souci. All rights reserved. Published by Scholastic Inc.

12 11 10 9 8 7 6 5 4 3 2 1   0 1 2 3 4 5/9

Printed in the U.S.A.   08

For my mother, Dorothy
                              —F.L.

For Noelle
          —D.D.S.

Once upon a time, in a palace beneath the sea,
there lived six beautiful princesses.
The youngest was the most beautiful of all.
She had skin as soft as rose petals
and eyes as blue as the deepest sea.
But like all the mermaids, she had no feet —
only a fish's tail.

Now, each mermaid had her own small garden.
The older sisters filled their gardens
with many things they found
when ships were wrecked at sea.

The youngest had nothing in hers
but a marble statue of a handsome boy.
It was the only thing she wanted.
She loved to look at the statue
and think about the world it came from —
the world above the water.

"What is it like up there?" she asked her grandmother.

"When you are fifteen you will see it all.
Then you will swim to the top of the water
and sit on the rocks in the moonlight.
You will see the ships and the people,
and you may sing to them
just like your sisters."

"It is lovely up there," her sisters told her.
"But there is no place more wonderful
than the bottom of the sea."

"I want to see for myself," said the little mermaid.

"You must wait," said her grandmother.

So the little mermaid waited.
Often she went to her own little garden
and stared at the statue of the handsome boy.

At last it was her fifteenth birthday.
"Come," said her grandmother,
"I will dress you like your sisters."
And she put a crown of pearls on her head
and strung pearls around her tail.
Then the little mermaid rose up through the water
as light as a bubble.

When she came to the top
she saw a big ship.
On the deck were many people,
but one stood out from all the rest.
He was a handsome prince
who looked like her statue
come to life.
The little mermaid could not take her eyes
off the prince.

Now, it was the prince's sixteenth birthday
and there was a grand party.
Everyone was singing and dancing.

The hours passed. Fireworks turned night into day.
Still the little mermaid did not move.
She kept on staring
at the handsome prince.

Suddenly, there was a clap of thunder
and a flash of lightning.
Wind blew.
The waves grew higher and higher.
And rain fell like stones on the water.

The big ship cracked in two
and began to sink.
People were thrown into the water.

"The prince!" thought the little mermaid.
"The prince must not drown!"

She dove into the sea
and swam to the prince.
His eyes were closed
but he was still breathing.
Holding his head above the water,
the little mermaid let the waves carry them
all through the night.

At dawn the storm was over.
The mermaid saw a great white building
near the shore.
It was a holy temple.
Around the temple was a garden.
The little mermaid swam toward the garden
and laid the prince on the sand near a palm tree.
Then she kissed his lips
and swam out behind some rocks.

"I will wait until someone comes to help him," she thought.

Soon a lovely girl came out of the building.
She ran to the prince.
Slowly he opened his eyes and smiled at her.
But he did not smile at the mermaid
for he did not know she had saved his life.

Sadly, the little mermaid dove down
to the palace beneath the sea.
She went to her garden
and flung her arms around the statue
of the handsome boy.
He looked so much like the prince.

"What did you see above the water?" asked her sisters.
But the little mermaid would tell them nothing.

Many nights she swam up to the place
where she had left the prince.

Yet she always returned sadder than before
because she never saw him.

Her only comfort was to sit in her garden
with her arms around the statue.

The little mermaid felt very unhappy.
At last she had to tell her sisters about the prince.
"Oh, little sister," one of them said,
"we know of this prince.
We can show you where he lives."
So the six sisters swam to the prince's palace.

The palace was built of shining stone
with marble steps leading down to the sea.

From then on, the little mermaid swam
near the palace every night.
Sometimes she saw the prince
standing alone on the balcony.
Sometimes she saw him on a ship.
Often she heard the sailors praise him
and she was glad she had saved him from drowning.

One day the little mermaid asked her grandmother,
"If human beings aren't drowned
  can they live forever?
  Don't they die as we do?"

"Yes," said her grandmother,
"they must die, too.
  And their lives are shorter than ours.
  We live three hundred years.
  Then we turn to foam on the water.
  But human beings have a soul
  that lives forever.
  And the soul rises up through the air . . .
  up . . . up . . . to the shining stars."

"Can I have a soul?" asked the little mermaid.

"If a human being married you,
you could have a soul.
But that is impossible," said her grandmother.

"Why?" asked the little mermaid.

"Because no human being would ever marry you.
People think your fish's tail is ugly.
Only legs are beautiful to them.
They don't know any better."

"Oh, I would give anything to be a human being!
I want to marry the prince,
and I want to have a soul that lives forever."

"You must forget that, my dear," said her grandmother.
"We have a much happier life down here."

But the little mermaid could not forget.

One day the little mermaid left the palace
and swam out through a strange forest.
She was going to find the old witch of the sea.
The witch was the only one who might help her.

The trees and bushes of the forest were half plant
and half animal.
Their slimy branches clung like giant worms
to everything they touched.
The little mermaid's heart beat fast with fear.
She was so frightened she almost turned back.
Then she thought of the prince and a human soul
and on she went.

Soon she came to a clearing
where she saw the house of the sea witch.
It was built from the bones of shipwrecked men.

There sat the sea witch
with water snakes crawling in her lap.

"I know what you want," said the sea witch.
"You want legs so the prince will love you.
 And you want a soul that lives forever."

"How did you know?" asked the little mermaid.

"I know everything," said the sea witch.
"You are not wise, my pretty one,
 but you shall have your way.
 It will only bring you trouble."
 The witch laughed a horrible laugh.

"I will give you a magic potion," she said.
"Before the sun rises, you must swim
 to land and drink it.
 Then your tail will split apart
 and you shall have legs.
 No dancer will be as graceful as you.
 But with every step, you will feel
 as if you are walking on sharp knives.
 Can you bear such pain?"

"I can," said the little mermaid.

"But remember this," said the sea witch.
"You can never become a mermaid again.
And if the prince does not marry you,
you will not win a soul.
The morning after someone else becomes his wife,
you will become foam on the sea.
Do you still want to drink the magic potion?"

"I do," said the little mermaid.

"Very well," said the sea witch. "But you must pay me.
No one has a sweeter voice than you.
I will take your voice as payment for my potion."

"If you take my voice, what will
I have left?" asked the little mermaid.

"You have beauty, grace, and eyes that speak
for you," said the witch. "That is enough."

"So be it," whispered the little mermaid.

And from that moment on,
she could no longer speak or sing.

At sunrise the little mermaid swam
to the shore near the prince's palace.
Quickly she drank the magic potion.
Then she felt a stab of pain
and she fainted on the sand.

When she opened her eyes
the prince stood beside her.
"Who are you?" he asked.

The little mermaid could not answer.
She could only look at him
with her dark blue eyes.

"Poor girl, can't you speak?"
asked the prince.
The little mermaid lowered her eyes
and shook her head.
"Do not worry," said the prince.
"I will take care of you."

The prince took the little mermaid's hand
and led her to the palace.
And with every step
she felt as if sharp knives were beneath her feet.

That night there was a splendid ball.
Dressed in a golden gown,
the little mermaid danced and danced.
Everyone was enchanted by her grace and beauty —
especially the prince.

Later, when the others were asleep,
the little mermaid walked down the marble steps
to cool her burning feet in the cold sea.
She heard her sisters singing sadly,
and she saw their long, beautiful hair
flowing in the breeze.
She waved to them
and they swam close to shore.
"We miss you, little sister," they told her.
"We will come to see you often
while the prince is sleeping."

The little mermaid grew dearer
to the prince with each passing day.
He loved her as if she were his sister.
But he never thought of making her his wife.

"You remind me of a lovely girl
who found me after a storm
and saved my life," the prince said.
"I have never seen her since,
yet she is the only one
who could ever be my wife.
But you and I will never part.
I promise you."

"Oh, if only I could speak," thought the little mermaid.
"If only I could tell him
that *I* am the one who saved his life.
I was hiding behind the rocks.
I saw the lovely girl
whom he loves more than me."
The little mermaid wanted to cry
but she could not. Mermaids have no tears.

Now it happened that the prince's parents
wished him to marry the daughter
of a neighboring king.
"I cannot love her," he told the little mermaid.
"But I must go and see the princess
and you will come with me.
I hope you are not afraid of the sea."
The little mermaid smiled.

The next morning the prince's ship sailed
into the harbor of the neighboring kingdom.
Trumpets blew,
church bells rang,
and the prince was welcomed to the city.

Every day there were balls and parties
in his honor.
But he did not see the princess.

"Our daughter has been staying
at a holy temple," said her father, the king.
"She is on her way and will be here soon."

At last the princess arrived.
The prince went in to meet her.
He could not believe his eyes.
"It is *you*," he said.
"You are the one who found me after the storm.
You, and only you, will be my wife."

On the day of the marriage
the little mermaid held the bride's wedding train.
She felt that her heart was breaking.
Soon she would die
and become foam on the sea.

That very night the prince and his bride
went on board the ship.
When it grew dark, lanterns were lit
and everyone danced.
The little mermaid danced, too.
And this time the pain in her heart was even greater
than the pain she felt with every step.

The party lasted until the full moon
was high in the sky.
Then everyone went to sleep.

The little mermaid looked out at the sea.
She saw her sisters rising to the top.
Their long, beautiful hair no longer flowed in the breeze.
It had been cut off.

"We had to give our hair to the sea witch
to save you from death," they told her.
"You have one last chance.
In exchange for our hair,
the witch gave us this knife.
Before the sun rises
you must kill the prince
whom you love the most.
When his blood spills over your feet,
you will become a mermaid again.
Hurry! Either you or he must die before sunrise."

The little mermaid drew back the curtains of the tent
where the prince and his bride were sleeping.
She bent down and kissed the prince.
She raised the sharp, shining knife,
which seemed to quiver in her hand.
But then...

She flung the knife far out to sea.
The waves gleamed red where it fell.
The little mermaid took one last look at the prince.
Then she threw herself from the ship
and felt her body turn to foam.

But the little mermaid was not dead.
When the sun rose,
she heard voices like music.
She saw hundreds of beautiful beings
floating through the air.

"I am floating, too," said the little mermaid
in a voice like the others.

"Yes," they told her.
"You have suffered enough.
You are one of us now.
We are spirits of the air.
Like you, we have no soul,
but we can win one."

"How?" asked the little mermaid.

"We fly to hot countries
  and bring cool breezes.
We spread the fragrances of flowers.
For three hundred years, wherever we go,
  we bring peace and happiness.
Then we win a soul,
  and you will, too."

For the first time
the little mermaid felt tears in her eyes.

She saw the prince and his bride.
They were staring sadly at the bubbling foam
as if they knew she had thrown herself into the waves.

Invisible now,
the little mermaid kissed the bride
and smiled at the prince.
Then, with the spirits of the air,
she floated away.